Sea, Sand, Me!

For Shelly

Sea, Sand, Me!
Text copyright © 2001 by Patricia Hubbell
Illustrations copyright © 2001 by Lisa Campbell Ernst
Manufactured in China
www.harperchildrens.com

Library of Congress Cataloging-in-Publication Data
Hubbell, Patricia.
    Sea, sand, me! / by Patricia Hubbell ; illustrated by Lisa Campbell Ernst.
        p.   cm.
    Summary: A young girl enjoys building sand castles, splashing in the sea,
and making a new friend during an afternoon at the beach.
    ISBN 0-688-17378-0 — ISBN 0-688-17379-9 (lib. bdg.)
    [1. Beaches—Fiction.   2. Stories in rhyme.]   I. Ernst, Lisa Campbell, ill.
II. Title.
PZ8.3.H848 Sg   2001   00-32011
[E]—dc21   CIP
                                                  AC

Typography by Elynn Cohen
8   9   10   ❖

Sea, Sand, Me!

by Patricia Hubbell

illustrated by Lisa Campbell Ernst

HarperCollins*Publishers*

Pack up our beach bags.
Load up the car.
We're going to the beach—

And here we are!

Flippy-floppy sun hat.
Wiggly-waggly toes.

Mommy rubbing lotion
On my nose, nose, nose.

Pail and shovel.
Dig, dig, dig.

Jump in, Dolly!
Jump in, Pig!

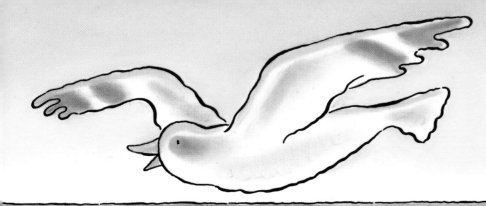

Beach day!
Beach day!
Sun. Sand. Sea.
Gulls squawk-squawking,
Talking just to me.

Somebody is coming . . .
Spoon in his hand!

We make a giant castle
In the scritchy-scratchy sand.

Seashell toenails.
Seaweed hair.

Lifeguard laughing
In his great tall chair.

Sand in our belly buttons.
Sand in our pants.
We jump in the water
And dance, dance, dance.

We jump, jump, jump
In the curly-whirly wave.
Cold water doesn't scare us
'Cause we're brave, brave, brave.

Beach day! Beach day!
Sea. Sand. *Wheeee!*

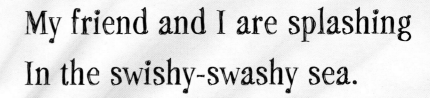

My friend and I are splashing
In the swishy-swashy sea.

Lunchtime! Lunchtime!
Cookies. Lemonade.

We flop on our blankets
In the shade, shade, shade.

We climb on the rocks.
See a starfish on a stone,
A little minnow swimming,
And a big fish bone!

We bounce our beach ball.
Put shells in our pails.

Wave at a boat
With big red sails.

Shadows on the sand now.
Sun hanging low.

We pack up our beach bags.
Home we go.

Beach day! Beach day!
Wish we could stay . . .
Hope I see my friend
On the next beach day.